Born

Sleepi

Miami University Press

ıg

H. C. Gildfind

Miami University Press

Oxford, Ohio

Copyright © 2021 by H. C. Gildfind

Library of Congress Cataloging-in-Publication Data

Names: Gildfind, H. C., 1981- author.

Title: Born sleeping / H. C. Gildfind.

Description: Oxford, Ohio : Miami University Press, [2021]

Identifiers: LCCN 2020032654 | ISBN 9781881163695

(trade paperback ; acid-free paper)

Subjects: LCSH: Interpersonal relations—Fiction. | Stillbirth—
Fiction. | Psychic trauma—Fiction. | LCGFT: Domestic fiction.

Classification: LCC PR9619.4.G544 B67 2021 | DDC 823/.92—dc23

LC record available at https://lccn.loc.gov/2020032654

Designed by Crisis

Printed on acid-free, recycled paper

in the United States of America

Miami University Press

356 Bachelor Hall

Oxford, Ohio 45056

No one ever told me that grief felt so like fear.

—C. S. Lewis, *A Grief Observed*

I

It's lunch time. You are both working from home today. You are both having a break. You are lying on the bed, listening to Ivan cook. There's the radio playing, low and constant. The dull thud of his chopping. The clink and clatter of metal on metal. His muted muttered swears at the dog who, you know, will be under his feet, shadowing him, a living trip-hazard awaiting the regular miracle of food falling from on high.

You are reading a funny book. When he answers the phone you are laughing out loud though some part of you already senses a new vibration in the air, which—you can feel it—is changing the air forever. It's coming from the tone of his voice: low, and lowering. It's coming from his single word answers. Yes. Okay. Yes. Okay. It's coming from the image of him when you get up and go to the kitchen: the slump of him. He looks different.

He puts the phone down. Resumes his cooking. He is moving strangely slow. You can see what has happened. This new vibration has transformed the air to liquid: to water, or mud; to treacle, or blood.

He doesn't look up as you push towards him. What's wrong?

He doesn't look up when you stand right next to him. What's happened?

Instead, he reaches for the pepper grinder. He slowly grinds the pepper into the pot. Puts the grinder down. Stirs the food.

You look at what he's made: a stir-fry. It smells delicious. Your stomach rumbles. Saliva squirts under your tongue. You are as sophisticated as a dog.

Staring at the food, he exhales heavily, shakily—melodramatically, you think, as a panic of irritation rushes through you. Then, he says it: They lost the baby.

Your face feels strange—smiling and wincing at once.

A weird sound blurts from you—a laugh. A laugh cut short by a single word: *What?*

Finally, he looks up. Though you are standing very close, and are now eye-to-eye, he is looking right through you at something else.

He turns back to the food. Again, he says it: They lost the baby. His voice sounds normal now, as if this shocking thing has already been diminished to the realm of ordinary fact.

You are slow to catch up. What do you mean *lost?*

Still, somehow, there's a smile—a laugh—in your voice. A weird, incredulous, angry laugh. You think: Ludicrous! You wonder: What sort of a sick joke is this?! You are still in the world of words, the world of books which you fill your life and head with to both connect yourself to—and distance yourself from—the hell that is other people. You are wondering, How do you *lose* a baby? How *careless*, to *lose* a baby!

It died, he says, absently pushing the food around the pan with a spoon. It died this morning.

Instantly, you glimpse what he has already seen: how a single moment in time can turn a baby—who has been He for months and months—into an It.

And already, you know it: something terrible has happened—something terrible, that you will never truly understand.

Nausea rushes through you. You breathe deeply, shoving the sickness down. You say, But we only saw them last week. They were ok. She said everything was "Awesome."

She had. She'd looked great, and she'd been ... boastful. That's how it seemed to you both, as you drove home afterwards, perplexed as ever by Mel and Stefan's shameless self-absorption, their shallowness, their—you agreed—narcissism. That night, once the four of you had moved from the restaurant to a café, and Ivan spoke to his brother and sister-in-law for the first time all evening, they'd automatically taken out their phones and started swiping so he was left talking to the crowns of their heads. Their rudeness was so blatant and extreme that it was almost funny. Almost. In reality, it was shocking—not because it was surprising, but because it was as typical and predictable as Ivan's resultant, and pathetic, hurt humiliation.

You'd stood up, excused yourself, and walked across the road to the bookshop. It was either that, or "making a scene." It was either that, or smashing their phones into their stupid fucking faces.

You'd both found it ugly, that night, how Mel had seemed to preen, as if the biological process unleashed within her was some sort of a personal triumph. If it was a triumph—and every pregnancy and baby does, indeed, seem miraculous to you—wasn't it a triumph of the blood and the bone, rather than the person?

Well, what would *you* know? And it was the very definite fact of your not knowing that seemed to load the subtext at the table that night as she acted as if—finally—she'd gotten one up on you. Perhaps she had.

Over the years, you've sensed that your value has been infuriatingly inexplicable to her. Though only ten years lie between you (as you approach forty, she thirty) you nevertheless seem to be utterly alien to her, a UFO: an Unidentifiable Female Object. So educated, but no cashed-up, fancy job. In a relationship forever, but no wedding, no marriage, no children—nothing at all, apparently, to show for it. No social life, at least not one proven by a stream of photos uploaded onto social media—taken from the endless carefully choreographed activities that she seems to fill her life with. But what must repulse Mel more than any of this is your utter failure to cultivate feminine beauty—for really, the only thing worse than an unidentifiable female object is an identifiably feminist one. *Gross!* She's hot and you're not—right? She's hot and you're—what?

Projection! Insecurity! That's what you accuse yourself of each time you notice your relish in shredding Mel to pieces like this—yet the credibility of your analyses seemed to grow with the size of her belly, especially when, at the café last week, she took out her phone and showed you her most recent Instagram post.

In the image, she stood in the archetypal "pregnant celebrity" pose: naked, turned side-on, one arm barely covering her engorged breasts whilst the other embraced her neat round belly.

Her phone, you presume, was propped on the bathroom sink, its camera on a timer. She was glamorously made up, her hair carefully styled, her skin—somehow—uniformly tanned. Of course she looked beautiful—she *is* beautiful—but that was despite the glamazon theatrics and the muck smeared all over her. Not sure what to do, you swiped the screen and ended up in a gallery of photos from the same selfie session. Endless pictures of her posing cutely, girl-next-doorishly, comically, pornographically. She watched you fumble. Seemed to enjoy the spectacle of your stumbling. Eventually, she rolled her eyes like a teen, took the phone back, swiped it to the original image, and returned it to you, apparently wanting some kind of comment.

What were you meant to say? The phrase "pregnant whore" darted through your mind—irrational, vicious. You looked at her. Looked back at the phone. Recalled similar images of Demi Moore, Kim Kardashian, Beyoncé. Mel was all of these women—and she was none of them. She was an imitation—a collage.

Your face burned. Why should *I*, you wondered, feel embarrassed by *her* exposure—*her* narcissism, *her* exhibitionism? You quickly realised that it wasn't just embarrassment that made you blush, but anger—anger at the obscure game she was playing—and another emotion too. Something less

7

clear, but deeper. Unease. Yes, Mel's performance—her confrontation—was unsettling something right at the hot bloody core of you.

It's just a dumb picture, you told yourself. It's just a dumb picture, taken by a dumb person, for dumb reasons.

But it wasn't just a picture, was it?

Underneath, you saw a strange list of words that you hadn't really registered at first because they were written in a language—a code—that you didn't understand the purpose or meaning of: #pregnantbelly #bodytransformation #momtobe #momsofinstagram #pregnantandperfect #fitpregnancy #pregnantyogi #sexybabybump #biglove #motivation #inspiration #instababy #instababe #influencer.

Influencer?

Suddenly, you felt very, very old and very, very stupid. #instaidiot, you thought, dully. #instabitch, you thought, vaguely aware that it was you now—and not she—who was illiterate.

Yes, it was definitely you, now, who was floundering in a language and a culture that meant absolutely nothing to you. Instagram, Facebook, Twitter. These digital mediums that are apparently so powerful they're not only reshaping public and political discourses, but also the very structure of the human brain. More powerful than books, so you've been told. More powerful than any bloody book on the planet.

You'd looked up at Mel's smug, expectant face, and realised that it wasn't just ten years that lay between you, but an entirely new world—one that you had shunned and avoided and denigrated without knowing a single thing about it.

You gazed again at the image of Mel's naked, bursting body—and the strange code beneath it—and you wondered: How is this worded, imaged thing so very different to the worded, image-full things that I create? Aren't we both just making fictions and casting them out into space—like astronomers sending messages to the stars—hoping for a connection? Unlike your attempts, though, Mel's bore proof of success: her single photo had won her 558 "likes" and 96 comments from all over the globe. Your stories, by contrast, disappeared into the world untethered and alone. Neither they, nor anyone else, reported back to you about their travels.

Once upon a time, this was exactly what you loved about printed texts: the mysterious, endless potential of their solitary journeys. But looking at Mel's post, last week, the unknowability of your stories' fates just seemed like silent proof that books are dead—dead because digital, consumable, tiny texts like hers are replacing them.

These thoughts winded you, and your inner recoil must have shown on your face for, when you looked at her again, Mel was beaming right back at you, her eyes gleaming under their glitter-smear of shadow.

As your eyes locked, you saw the true nature of what was happening at that café table. Mel was feeling powerful—and she was revelling in that feeling. She was the bearer of the first grandchild. She knew the beauty and potency of her young, pregnant body. And she fully believed, too, that her fertility and glamorous image had more power than any of your carefully crafted sentences ever would.

You recoiled further. Mel's power was real—as real as the heat you felt radiating from her skin where your arm lay alongside hers on the table.

For a moment, you were so disoriented that you couldn't look at her, or the photo.

Instead, you stared across the table at Ivan. He was still trying to talk to his brother. Stefan was still playing with his phone.

You recited to yourself the understanding that you've spent your entire adult life trying to get your head around.

There's the power that you know you have.

There's the power that you have, but don't realise you have.

There's the power that you think you have, whether you have it or not.

There's the power others think you have, whether you have it or not.

There's the power *to* ...

There's power *over* ...

Such ordinary, simple little words—yet their arrangement dictates your relationship to yourself, to others, to everything.

In that moment, on that night, you saw how—unlike you—Mel knew *exactly* where her power lay. She knew it, and she had weaponised it through an image on a phone.

You looked at her victorious face. You thought of Nietzsche's Superman, and you wondered, What would he think about *this* creature—this Superwoman?

Luckily, then, the sharp and entwined feelings that Mel usually provokes in you reasserted themselves, blasting away the fog of your confusion and the embarrassment of your recoil. The first feeling? That familiar desire to protect her. And the second? The desire to slap the shit right out of her.

Unable, or unwilling, to act on either impulse, you smiled with—you felt it—the pressed lips of a disapproving school marm. You pushed the phone towards her across the table. She smiled, her eyes sparkling with glee, apparently mistaking your bitten-down look for jealousy. You let her mistake it. If that was what she needed, it was no loss of yours. As Ivan says, whenever you let loose on the pair of them: We've had every opportunity—she hasn't. We have so much more than they do. And they're heaps younger than us. We're from different worlds.

This is true. It was you, after all, who originally came up with this catalogue of excuses when you first felt the tectonic shifts that your differing choices and chances were creating—shifts that were carving up his family, cleaving open the cracks that had already been made by the cultural differences you and Mel had stormed into his parents' non-Australian, non-Anglo home. But so what? That's your reply to such excuses these days. So. Bloody. What. Your *brother,* you reply, has had every opportunity, but he seems pretty happy setting the bar low—for the *both* of them. He seems pretty happy underestimating her, just as everyone *else* has always underestimated her. I guess it's not very threatening for *him* to make a life with someone who aspires to be nothing more than a Real Housewife, *right*?

You've always assumed that she—a rural kid, who struggled at school—

thinks that everyone *else* thinks she's Dumb White Trash, a Bogan, a Country Bumpkin. You've always assumed that being "hot" is what has been reified and rewarded in her home and her schooling and beyond. You've assumed her high school friends have all had children, by now, and are feeding her an endless ream of carefully staged images of #hotmamas and #cutebubbas and #happyfamilies. You've assumed, too, that she's been unable or unwilling to resist what her friends and family—and the celebrity culture she is so enamoured with—has posited as ideal. You've assumed a lot of things—haven't you?—but then again, Mel actually did say, once, that she'd *love* to become one of those repulsive, Botoxed, liposucked, re-filled, fake-titted, makeup-slathered, fame-seeking housewives from the TV show. *Anyone*, you've ranted, can do better than that!

Ivan, exasperated, embarrassed—by you, or them, or himself?—and averse to conflict in any form, always ends such outbursts in the same way: It's *their* life—*their* business. Don't be such a snob.

What he means, of course, is: Don't be such a bitch. That's what he means—whether he agrees with you or not. Well, you *are* a snob, you *are* a bitch, and you're beyond pretending otherwise. So. Bloody. What.

But all of that was way back then.

All of that was last week, and all the weeks and months and years before today.

This is now, when you and Ivan are standing in a kitchen, feeling how this strange new thing has—in the space of a phone call—drawn a deep line in the dirt of your shared histories, severing the future from the past by turning your stories into "before then" and "after that."

We only saw them last week, you repeat. She looked so *good*. She said everything was *fine*. She was *strutting*.

Ivan doesn't answer. He just stares down at the food he's made.

You go back to the bedroom. Sit on the side of the bed. Pick up the book you were reading and lay it in your lap. You stroke its glossy cover and try to distract yourself from the sickening feeling in your throat. You don't realise, yet, that this feeling will stay with you forever—that it will live inside you, waiting for all sorts of obscure things to trigger it to life. You haven't understood, yet, that memories are grown just like any other part of your body—just like bones and hair and nails—grown from the bits and pieces of the world that enter and pass through you.

You return to the kitchen. He's still staring into his pot. What happened?

He shrugs. Half shakes his head. Turns off the cooker. Sets about doing things with plates and cutlery.

You ring his mother's workplace. The woman who picks up the phone interrogates you. You explain, I'm her son's partner. She says, *Who?* Frustrated, you call yourself what you always refuse to call yourself: I'm her daughter-in-law. The woman puts you straight through.

When Petra answers there is no Hello—and no hesitation. There is just a wail. Just a terrible, gutting wail.

This woman of composure and restraint—of pride and repression—cannot stop herself.

Her pain rockets through you, icing your skin. She is hours away, but through this tiny phone she is filling your head, the room, the house and the endless fields and forests and skies outside your window. Primal love, primal pain, primal grief. These inarticulable things you know nothing about—these inarticulable things you don't *want* to know about. For once, you want to help Petra rather than defend yourself against her—but even as you understand this, you know that nothing in the world can shield her from what has just happened.

Shaky, breathing silence. Then, again, she wails. Another sensation shudders through you: an overwhelming sense of recognition. This sound she's making? It's the same animal sound you've heard thousands make on the nightly news. It's the same sound that makes you turn the nightly news off. It's the sound of total disbelief, helplessness and shock. It's the sound of a body and mind falling into an abyss of total, irrevocable, undeniable loss.

As you listen to her, you sense that new feeling sickening your throat again—that lump, like a stray tooth, rooting itself deeper as each new moment passes through you.

Finally, Petra is quiet. She blows her nose, gets her breath back. Then she begins to talk and talk and talk. She speaks very quickly, as if her brain has already begun the impossible work of processing what's happened, already trying to make sense of this inexplicable, random assault of events. She's looking for causes and effects, beginnings and endings, chronology—

meaning. She recounts how, only yesterday, her workmates held a special party for all the grandmas-to-be in the factory. There were four of them—"Four of us!"—all waiting for new babies, all of them first-time grandmas. Together, her friends had sewn her a beautiful, quilted blanket.

Petra pauses in her telling. She says it again, They made me a special blanket, to wrap him in. They made me a blanket—to hold him in. They made me a special blanket...

She stops for a second, as if staring down the new reality that these repetitions can only, now, return her to. After a moment, she starts talking again—fast—repeating the story of what has happened so far.

Stefan called her early this morning, and said: "When Mel woke up, he wasn't moving." Then Stefan cried and cried and cried. Then he hung up. He just left Petra, like that, shocked to the core. Confused. Disbelieving. She doesn't know what has happened. She just knows that the baby must be dead. It's *so* unfair! she wails. It's *so* unfair, to have come *so* far. To have come *so* close. It's so unfair.

You remember your father being diagnosed with cancer. You remember protesting that it wasn't fair. He'd seemed genuinely puzzled by this, and replied, "What's *fairness* got to do with it?" You'd found strange comfort in this. You were impressed by his stoic calm.

Your mother was diagnosed with cancer a few years later. She refused to accept what was happening to her. She cried. She erupted with grief and terror and anger. "What have I done to deserve this? What have I done to deserve *this?*" Your father's reply—"Nothing"—only wounded her more.

For years, you thought your father's attitude was right, but eventually you realised that it derived less from noble logic than from the fact that his illness was treated by magic drugs whose only side effect was to keep him alive. Your mother's illness, however, had to be bombarded by the medieval tortures of chemotherapy, radiotherapy and the scalpel. In other words, whilst your father's brush with death was abstract, hers was not: his attitude proved less a triumph of logic than a total failure to empathise.

Eventually, his pills lost their magic powers. He got very sick, very quickly. Neither you nor your mother disagreed with him when he protested that he was too young to die. Neither you nor your mother argued with him when he cried that no one—*no one*—deserved the hell he was in. Instead, you did your best to make him comfortable as he learned, the hard way, that the stoic and rational are cruel vain liars when it comes to the lived terrors of the mind and the body.

It's so unfair, Petra says again, her voice gone quiet and flat and far away. So unfair...

And she's right. The death of a baby is not fair. A baby is conceived in order to grow. It grows in order to be born. And it is born in order to live—and keep on living.

Petra starts talking again. She describes how her workmates knew, straight away, that something was very wrong. Says they're sitting with her until her husband, Aleks, arrives. Says they've surrounded her like female bodyguards. You're like Gaddafi! you joke without thinking. She laughs. Together, you laugh. Then her laughter tumbles back to tears and then, again, those terrible wails. You tell her you're so, so sorry. You don't know what else to say, and you find yourself echoing the words she sobs down the phone. Awful, she sobs. Awful, you repeat. Terrible. Terrible. Shocking. Shocking. Horrible. Horrible. Eventually, she is quiet. Both of you listen to each other breathe. It's strange, how it's not embarrassing breathing together like this. Any other time there's been a silence between you, it has been loaded with all sorts of things neither of you have been willing or able to say.

Suddenly she whispers, I don't know what to say to them. Even lower, she whispers, I don't know what to *say* to them. The tone in her voice surprises you. What is it? She almost sounds frightened.

Then she is wailing again, as loud and uncontrollable as ever. You know, if she doesn't, that her body is saying the one thing—the only thing—that anyone can say.

When she is quiet, you promise her that you'll call back soon. You press the screen on the phone. Petra is gone. You feel nothing but a pure and luxuriant relief as distance silently resumes its place between you. It's not just the distance you've enforced by moving out here, but the distance you've always felt from people. You can feel these two different types of distances combining. You can feel them amplifying each other, transforming what has happened from a real thing into a thought thing—into nothing more than a story.

Ivan has finished serving out the lunch. Surprisingly, the food tastes delicious and, though you still feel nauseous, you stuff it down, as if your body thinks this might help you dislodge and swallow the lump forming in your throat.

As you eat, your mind roves over all that has happened in the past hour, your thoughts moving faster and faster, propelled by one clear—undeniable—feeling: excitement. This is a drama. This is an unusual and extreme event. This is a tragedy. You are disgusted with yourself, but your disgust dissolves when you think what you often think: Everyone rubbernecks at a car crash. *Everyone.*

You remind yourself there is pain being felt by people you are meant to care about. You try hard to feel it too: but you can't make yourself feel others' pain, just as you can't make yourself care for people that you don't. Instead—sitting across from your partner, eating the delicious food that he has cooked in the home that you both love—you feel a savage gratitude. Yes, you feel *glad*. *Glad*, that you've missed this bullet. *Glad*, because of your vague, barely-admitted superstition that there is only so much tragedy going around in this world—and a chunk of it has just been used up by *them* and not *you*. You've had your share of bad luck. Bad enough for you to know that trauma doesn't provide grist for the mill. Trauma damages the mill: what doesn't kill you makes you weaker. You've had enough bad luck to know that it's only the people on the outside of trauma who can make something of it. And that is where you and Ivan are at this very moment: on the outside. Thank God. Thank God. Thank God.

Are you okay?

Ivan shrugs. I don't feel anything, he says quietly. What *should* I feel?

You eat in silence for a while. Eventually you say what you think you're meant to say—what you don't want to say. We should be there. We should drive back. We should go, right after this.

Should. Should. Should. For years you have been disciplining yourself to steer clear of the innumerable sinkholes of "should" that seem to pock the landscape of every relationship. Sinkholes shaped by others, that you've wasted far too much of your life falling into and then struggling—blindly—to get out of again. Sinkholes that seem especially designed for women—for you have noticed that Ivan is seldom expected to think, feel or do any of the things your so-called friends and family have overtly, or covertly, expected of you.

He looks up, frowning. Why? He almost sounds angry. Why should we go back? There's nothing we can do.

You think: He's right. You say: We should go back for your parents—not for Mel and Stefan. They'll want to be left alone, won't they? They'll want privacy now—and afterwards—won't they?

You see them—that cocky, attractive young couple—returning to their modest little house in their rough-cut, outer suburb. You picture them walking into the plush, cream-tinted, low-lit nursery they'd recently finished: you've seen it—it was lovely. You remember how that little room felt like a living thing, its very air as swollen with expectant waiting as Mel's body. You imagine their empty-handed arrival. You feel the room instantly transform into something as sterile and void as a mock-up in a furniture shop—changing, in a single second, from a living thing to a dead thing. Places, you think, places *know* us. You've always felt this. Places, like animals, see and know everything about us.

Afterwards? Afterwards they'll have to go home, pack up the nursery and put everything away. Perhaps someone will do it for them—so they don't have to face it. Perhaps it will be stored somewhere, so they can use it next... unthinkable thought. Perhaps they will sell it all—or give it away. But would anyone even want those things? Won't their very newness taint them like an invisible stain, silently declaring all that happened—and all that didn't? You suddenly remember the world's supposedly shortest story: "For sale: baby shoes, never worn." As if anyone could ever—would ever—buy such a thing.

You think of Mel's Instagram and Facebook posts. You picture her triumphant face as she showed you the images and all the attention and praise they'd won from the ether. Now, you feel the pressure of that same audience—a global diaspora of real and virtual friends, family, workmates, acquaintances and countless, total strangers. You realise that—worse than packing up the nursery—is how Mel and Stefan will have to explain themselves to everyone. Again and again, they will have to explain to people what has happened. Instagram, or not, these things are always public—aren't they? Because you cannot hide a pregnancy—can you? You cannot hide a dead baby—can you?

A long, long time ago, in Scotland, your grandmother left her house, with her husband, to give birth to her third baby. He took her to a Catholic maternity home and left her there. When she told the nuns that the baby was coming, they scolded her. They told her that she wasn't ready to give birth. They might never have had sex, let alone a baby, but they'd *delivered* thousands. Plus, God was on their side, so who was she to argue?

Your grandmother gave birth alone. She baptised her daughter in a sink—then held her close as she died. The baby was buried somewhere on the grounds, anonymously, like a dog. The nuns refused to tell your grandmother where. Instead, they told her it was "God's will," and sent her home.

Your grandfather came to pick her up. He never said a word about it. They returned home to their two daughters who also knew, somehow, that they must never say a word about it—though their bodies spoke for them: one girl started wetting the bed, though she was ten years old; the other acquired a lazy eye, her iris spontaneously propelled inwards by a subconscious that was protesting in fright at the dark new atmosphere which cloaked and choked their home. Neighbours, friends, and family never said a word about it either. Everyone just carried on. Apparently, nothing had happened—though everything had changed.

The strange thing was, the older your grandmother got, the more this dead baby haunted her, as if the closer she was to death, the more she understood the power of ghosts. She'd find a way to divert every conversation towards the child, though when she did she'd get so *angry*—as if it were somehow you, or your siblings', or your parents' fault that she'd never been allowed to talk about it. It was your elder brother who seemed to understand her compulsive story-telling the most. He said she was seeking witness: she wanted the world to know that this terrible thing had happened, and that it mattered.

Your brother was right, in part, but over the years you sensed that what she really needed was a judge and jury to give her the definitive verdict: "It was not your fault." Of course, everyone reassured her of this in her later years, saying these exact five words whenever she needed to hear them—and she always needed to hear them. Eventually you realised there was only one person whose verdict she'd value. Not yours, not your family's, not her dead husband's. Not even the nuns who *were* witnesses to what happened, and who may well have been responsible for that baby's death. It was the verdict of the dead child that she needed the most—the verdict of Annie, her baby, whose name and story she made sure everyone knew before she herself died.

No. You cannot hide a pregnancy. You cannot hide a dead baby.

You cannot hide the presence of such absences.

You've both finished eating. You stand. You pick up Ivan's plate and cutlery. Looking down at him, you say, Your parents need us. They'll be heartbroken. They'll be in shock. But there's no conviction in your voice: you are hoping he will, once again, talk you out of your shoulds.

Instead, you both agree that, for now, you will ring Petra every hour or so to see how she is—to see what she wants—and to find out exactly what happened this morning. You'll keep on ringing her for updates—as if she's at a footy game and you want to know the score. You'll tell her that you're ready to do anything. Go straight to them. Stay away. Ring and ring and ring.

And in the meantime? What else is there to do but carry on with your work?

When you go to your desk, you glimpse the simple, devastating fact that will enlarge and overwhelm you over the next few days, then weeks, then months and years as more and more things happen to you and all the people that you know. Just another terrible cliché, proven true: life goes on. No matter what, life goes on and on and on—utterly indifferent to what it does to you.

Darwin was right: adapt or die. For most people, almost anything can be normalised. For most people, almost anything can be lived with, or around, or besides—or wherever it is that people live in relation to the holes ripped out of them. People cope, and they cope, and even if they can't cope they—mostly—keep on living.

After a couple of hours' work, you hear him talking in the other room, ringing his mother. You can barely discern his words, but the rhythm of their conversation fills the house: plodding, heavy, relentless. This is the weight and pace of the story Petra has begun to tell—for herself, and for others—within the larger story of her family.

You get up from your desk, wander down the hall, and stand in the doorway to his study. He looks up briefly, stares through you, and then looks back down at the floor, nodding and aha-ing. From his responses, you work out that his mother and father are at the hospital, waiting. (But what is there to wait for now? Or are they, really, holding vigil without realising it—without yet admitting it?) From Ivan's responses, you work out that Mel's parents have just arrived.

The lump in your throat grows a little, hardens, as this new understanding layers itself upon the others. Another surge of nausea flushes through you. How could you forget about *her* parents?

They live inland, hours away from the city, in a drought-struck farming region. You've never met them, and yet, somehow, you can see them so clearly. How can this be? But of course: you've heard Mel talk about them many times. Without irony, she'll complain: "Mum talks too much. Sometimes you've just gotta walk out the room. Nothing shuts her up. It's like there's something *wrong* with her. And dad's really quiet. But they kind of match, it's weird. He just *loves* her. You can just *tell*. The way he *looks* at her—and follows her 'round like a fucking *dog*. We tease him about it all the time. When he had to sell the farm, he went even more quiet. Like really, really, *really* quiet. We thought he was depressed. You know, one of those idiots who shoves a gun down their throat just 'cos they've lost their job. He kept disappearing into the workshop. Mum *freaked*. She wouldn't leave him alone. She thought he was going to string himself up, like Uncle Jake. She was gonna have some sort of *intervention*—like something from *Dr Phil*. She's such an *idiot*. Anyway, turns out he was just secretly making her this *love* seat, for their thirtieth anniversary. He's *always* making stuff for her—for all of us. Both of them are like that. Always doing stuff for people whether they want it done or not. Drives me fucking *nuts*."

It's from such monologues, and other scraps of information, that you've conjured a distinct image of these two middle-aged strangers. The mother is tall and slim. She is wiry and wired, energetic, always moving. Her hair (like her three daughters') is always bleached and ironed and carefully styled, and her clothes (like her three daughters') are always as fashionable as she can afford. She's an outwards person, a person who can't stop, a person who's always trying to outrun her thoughts and feelings by keeping her hands full and her feet moving.

The father is small. He's lean and brown and sinewy from years of working under a scorching sun. He's evasive, shy—never looks people in the eye. He walks stiffly, awkwardly—bone-sore from a lifetime of labouring—and, though he's retired, he still wears the same faded work-clothes he's worn for the entirety of his adult life. He's an inwards person. He plods on, forcing thoughts from his head by doing things that demand the immediacy and quiet of total concentration: working with big powerful animals; working with deadly machines and tools.

Obviously, what this husband and wife have in common is a compulsive need to keep themselves busy, to distance themselves from themselves through work and other people.

Obviously, their differences complement and unite them. Her noise and energy are a refuge from the quiet, monotone pressure that would otherwise build up and up inside of him. His quietness, his stillness—which everyone, except his wife, takes for calmness—relieves her from the noisy energy that constantly fizzes through her. These are the people you've conjured from Mel's relentless, affectionate bitching.

You imagine them this morning, asleep in the house they built to raise their six children in. You imagine them lying side by side, each with a hand upon the other, making sure that the other is there. You gaze at them, then hear—no, feel—the sound of that too-early phone call ripping open the dawn with the promise of news.

What will they think, in the few seconds between waking and picking up the phone? Will they say, She's given birth! And why not? Mel was, as she'd said, "ready to pop." Or, will they sense something else? Will the mother snap awake after an inexplicably fitful sleep and know, just *know*, something has happened to her child—to this part of her body that lives outside of her body? Either way, nothing will prepare her for the blunt, brutal fact that the phone will deliver to them: your baby's baby is dead.

How did they react to the news? Did they cry, inconsolably, as Petra did? Surely not. They'd have focused on getting to Mel as quickly as possible. They'd have gotten dressed, gone straight to the car and then pointed themselves towards the coast. What a drive that must have been. Did they talk as the hours and kilometres carried them from the tinder-dry fields of their home, to the distant, sky-scraped city? No. You can't see them talking. You see them, instead, sitting very calmly and quietly, perhaps letting the radio fill the silence gaping between them, neither of them daring to say anything other than what needed to be said when they stopped for petrol and coffee and toilet breaks. Surely they'd have known, automatically, that the grief must be postponed until after they'd seen with their own eyes that their daughter was safe—and their grandson was dead. Till then, you imagine, they wouldn't have believed any of it. You don't believe it yet either.

You walk into Ivan's study and perch on the edge of his desk. He puts a finger over his lips, then puts the phone on speaker so Petra's voice fills the room. Mel's mother has, you gather, taken control. This other mother must be asking all the questions that no one has yet dared to ask, questions a migrant tongue and migrant ear would find hard to ask sensitively—let alone understand the answers to. What happens to the baby's body? Are they meant to have a funeral—is that what people do? What happens to *Mel's* body? Will she be ok? (And will the other mother dare to ask, Why did this happen? What—or whom—is responsible? How often are such questions asked when people are floundering in disbelief and pain? How often are such questions asked when ordinary people are faced with the automatic, pervasive authority of doctors?)

You have never understood how women recover from pregnancy and giving birth. Only recently have you begun to learn from friends and family that many of them don't. Instead, their bodies and minds remain permanently altered by things they can barely describe. One of your friends is plagued by nightmares of her only child's labour, a labour where some sadistic doctor refused to give her pain relief. She was terrified. She thought she was going to die. That's not an exaggeration: she thought she was *dying*. You don't know how to help her. All you can do is let her talk about it as much as she needs to, because her mother—and other mothers—don't want to hear about it. They tell her it's normal. They tell her to "get over it." They even tell her to "get over it" by having another baby. They tell her to be grateful that she and her child are okay—even though, clearly, she is not okay at all.

You and Ivan keep listening to Petra. You see her being shoved aside by Mel's mother. You see this other woman striding into the ward that, you are learning, is kept especially for mothers of dead babies. You see her striding straight into that cemetery—built into the heart of the women's hospital—and you see her taking control. She will ask her questions without emotion. She will be professional. She will insist, patiently, that all of her questions are answered. She will not be ignored. She will not compromise or flinch until she has done everything within her power to understand what has happened to her daughter—and to protect her from whatever might happen next. She will ignore the grief that is filling her up inside, for she must not be toppled yet. She will take control of all that she can—using her body and her voice to build a buffer between her daughter's torture and everyone else's—and she will do this every day, from now on, until her daughter can do it for herself.

Petra keeps talking. Now that she's had a chance to gather the newly-broken pieces of herself—now that she's gained a couple of hours' distance from that first, blind-siding shock—she is doing what she always does when in company: she is recounting every single tiny detail of what she has seen and done and noticed. Even if you could not hear her, you'd know this from Ivan's slumped posture and the vacant look on his face—his habituated "tune out" from his parents' interminable monologues. You have never understood why they do this. Don't they see how people react when talked to—talked *at*—in this way? You've tried to give them the benefit of the doubt. Perhaps they're just shy, anxiously trying to make conversation in a language that is still foreign to them. (But they do it in their own language, too. You've watched them with their sons, with their friends.) Perhaps they are, simply and genuinely, interested in the minutiae of their own and others' lives. Perhaps they are terrified of silence, and so they try to fill it, feeling—as you often do yourself—that any awkwardness is somehow their fault. But listening, now, to the impenetrable rhythm of Petra's voice, you wonder if it's something else altogether. Is she, perhaps—like Mel's mother—building a wall with words? Is she, perhaps, a master in building worded-walls to shield herself and her loved ones from the terrifying experience of experiencing? Even you—especially you—can understand this. You've built your entire life through such worded means—though what have you ever, really, needed shielded from?

Nothing, compared to many people. Nothing, compared to Petra.

Petra and her family are refugees. You used to ask Petra what it had been like to flee her home with nothing other than her husband and two young sons, leaving one terrible unknown for another. You wanted to know how people survive such losses, such *fear*. You wanted to know how, in mid-life, someone starts all over again in a new country with an alien language and culture. It sounded terrifying to you—impossible—and you wanted to know the truth of it.

She would talk a little, but then she'd stop, dismiss it all with a shrug and say (shifting to the present tense, as if this grammatical move could obliterate the past): "It's fine. It's *fine!*" One day, she told you about the last time that she saw her mother and father. She told them that she and her family were going on a "holiday" because to tell them their plans, and to say goodbye, would put everyone in danger—not only from the authorities, but from the flooding, paralysing emotions that she was already, instinctively, learning to repress. She told you how, without saying goodbye (though everyone, except the children, knew what "holiday" meant), she abandoned her aging parents and fled. She left them to survive alone in a warzone and die alone in a ruined city. They were buried by strangers. She cut herself short, ended her story with a shrug and, though her eyes swam dangerously, said, "It's fine. It's *fine.*"

You no longer ask her about any of it. Ivan doesn't ask either, though you've warned him a million times: "They'll be dead, sooner or later, then you'll never know what really happened to them—which means you'll never know what really happened to *you.*" You've stopped pressuring him too, though, because you know that your motives are questionable (curiosity, voyeurism) and because you realised that your questions were picking at a scab that Petra had spent years growing. You'd realised the obvious, that when she said, "It's fine," what she meant was, "I can't talk about this. I don't want to talk about this. Please don't make me talk about this." And perhaps that's why she talks and talks and talks about everything else.

Finally, Ivan ends the call. He says, She sounds fine. She sounds normal. He apparently thinks that, because she sounds like her old self, she is her old self, even though—clearly—she will never be her old self ever again. He repeats her instruction: you should not visit yet. He says he agrees with her. Says he believes her. He is stupid—stupid on purpose.

As usual, your relief is so much greater than the guilt that flashes through you as you recognise—and reject—what you are expected to do: you should go anyway—to show that you care, to show that you know that this is important.

But you don't really care, do you? And Ivan? Does he *care*, really?

Over the years you've come to believe that some things, the important things, must be *felt* in order to be *known*. When you were younger you condemned your popular culture's privileging of feeling over thought, but now you recognise that such condemnations were never yours at all. They were the condemnations of the Father—of your father, and of all the men in your culture and history who compulsively boom that reason and rationality are the only way to know anything worth knowing. Now that you are older, you see those men for what they were and are: terrified children who cannot face what their feelings tell them about themselves and the world around them.

You ask yourself, If it were *me* and *my* baby? I'd want to be left alone, wouldn't I?

Probably. Most definitely.

But this isn't about you and your imaginary baby, is it? It's about real people you cannot know the insides of.

It's about real things you've never wanted anything to do with.

Oh, you think (your usual refrain), Who's to say what's right and wrong? Certainly not people like me. Certainly not people like us. Certainly not people who are stupid—stupid on purpose.

You spend the rest of the day doing ordinary things. It turns out to be, in fact, a lovely day. The weather is perfect. You are getting along. You each do your work and you are each working well for a change: normally one of you is up, while the other is down. Today, you don't snark and snipe at each other. Your emotions seem blunted, softened—perhaps they've simply retreated.

And, of course, there is an ominous darkness shadowing the day that, by sheer contrast, makes everything seem clearer and brighter and simpler and more beautiful than ever before.

It is now late in the afternoon. You, Ivan and the dog are walking along the creek to the waterfall. It fills you up, this place—this beloved place of fields and forest, plants and animals, and an infinite sky that never ceases to relieve you from your own stupid self. You breathe it all in, smelling and tasting the rich, sweet pungency of nature's perpetual mucky work going on around you.

Oh, shut up, you think. What kind of an idiot idealises nature? A dead baby is no less natural than a live one, is it? Women dying with dead babies stuck in them is the most natural thing in the world.

Once in a while, one of you says something. You agree that you cannot know it. You can only know an *idea* of what has happened. An abstraction. How can it be anything else? It's impossible to believe. Yes, life and death really are so scary—so cruel, so random.

What else is there to say apart from such stupid clichés?

As you walk, you feel it all unfurl in you. And what a shapely thing it is, this dead baby's story. But no—that's not quite right. The contours and curves lie in the story that loops *around* the dead baby, for a baby that hasn't lived can't have a story, can it? Its beginning *is* its end, its life transformed into a moment in time: a life-death. Less a novel, than a short story. Less a short story, than a vignette. Less a vignette—a scene—than a sentence. That sentence: "For sale: baby shoes, never worn."

But that's not quite right either, is it? For everyone *else* this baby's death might just be a moment in time. But not for the baby. Not for the man and woman that dreamed of him, planned for him, conceived him. Not for the mother that carried him and carefully, lovingly, made a nursery for him. Not for the father that spent months replying with his lips and palms to the strange Morse code kicked through his partner's ever-stretching belly. And not for the grandparents, either, whose entire lives and selves seem written in tribal blood.

Well, you are not them. In this scenario, you belong to the group called "everyone else"—that is, the people for whom this baby's death might simply act as a blank slate onto which your own stories can be written. For us, this baby's death might, in fact, be reduced to little more than a literary device. Without a narrative arc of his own, he will, instead, play a role in the narrative arcs of the living. He will become a plot-point marking change—or a refusal to change. His death might become a metaphor or a symbol, something used to signify something other than itself: a punishment; a warning; a sacrifice. (But of whom? For what?) He will most certainly become a structural device—an organiser of narrative time—a singular moment when numerous people's stories stop and intersect before (just as suddenly) moving unstoppably away, into the future, forever leaving him behind.

That phrase—"leaving him behind"—hits you, follows you, attaches itself to the rhythm of your stride. It sounds so cruel, but it also sounds funny because—really!—how *careless* can someone be?! You recall your initial reaction to Ivan's news, just this morning. The ludicrous *hilarity* of it. How do you *lose* a baby? How *clumsy*, to lose a baby! And now, *Where's* your baby?! I left him behind. Oopsy daisy! What do you mean, "left him behind?" Where?! In the *past*, silly!

You walk quietly alongside Ivan and your dog as the story continues to shift about inside you, finding—making—its place. If you were to write it, how would you approach it? Anyone would think its tragic and true nature would guarantee its relevance and power—but you know such traits might be its greatest weakness. It has taken years for you to learn that profound life experiences—and the big questions they provoke—are best approached crabwise, best squinted at sidelong. This is how you avoid getting overwhelmed. This is how you see that such big events are only, in the end, constituted by tiny details and subtle shifts. The writer's job is to describe these glimpses and moments *precisely*: that's all. This is how writers help readers to articulate and challenge their own experiences. It is *not* a writer's job to entertain with titillating tricks that deny the complexity of reality.

But *this* baby's death is not a trick. This baby's death *is* the reality. Doesn't this *matter*? Doesn't this realness permit you—perhaps even oblige you—to use it in a story? Or will storying its death automatically reduce it to an obvious, predictable, and thus melodramatic literary device?

You recall a gnarly old professor-writer who, in lieu of opening introductions, simply announced to your workshop group: "Let me tell y'all something. The writer is always, always the *stupidest* person in the room." He savoured your communal flinch, as you each recognised the truth in what he said: why else did you all scurry home each night, baffled and scared, trying to make sense of things via words on a page? Later, in a one-to-one meeting, he drawled at you: "You know what you keep sayin' in workshop? 'It's too obvious.' But some things just *are* obvious. Most of your goddamn *life* is obvious. Without obviousness there's no way *in* to a story. Without obviousness, you can't make layers—layers of *meaning*—d'you know what I *mean*?"

Perhaps, after all, you know as much about writing as you do about life: nothing. Perhaps you are confusing "good writer" with "*literary* writer"— that is, the kind of writer most people cannot stand to read. Perhaps there is something fundamentally wrong with values that disallow you from writing about real things that matter to real people—which brings you to a related issue: appropriation. You think: This is not *my* story to tell. I must not be one of those writers who feed on the pain of others.

Suddenly, falling from way up on high, a cool, eerie cry drops through the air like a stone. And again, then again. Simultaneously, you and Ivan stop and look up. There, he says, spotting the bird through the canopy. It's so high up that its two-metre wingspan has been reduced to a small black squiggle. There, you say, a second later, spotting its mate through the canopy on the other side of the sky (these otherwise solitary birds are always, always paired). For a moment you watch the wedgetails surf the thermals. Surely no one, you think, pays more careful, loving attention to the dead than the predators and scavengers who feast upon them?

Still looking up, you notice the plants sprouting from the surrounding gums' upthrust trunks and outstretched limbs: epiphytes, or parasites, using the mammoth trees to find sunlight. Ha! The pissed-off professor was right. The truth *is* obvious: it lies right in front of you, most of the time. Look, here is the truth—lying—in plain sight! Those eagles and these plants are doing nothing other than reminding you that the ecosystems of the world—including the cultures that grow and die upon it—depend upon relationships that are seldom chosen and cannot, always, be differentiated: symbiosis, parasitism, predation.

Ivan starts walking again. You tug the dog's lead, follow him.

Maybe your concerns are just excuses, an eloquent means of denying that you're just not up to the task of writing because, in reality, there are many ways to deal with literary and ethical quandaries. You could, for example, completely ignore them: irrespective of what others might think, *you* know that your stories are painstakingly crafted fictions. Also, you could deal with the issue of appropriation by refusing to usurp the parents' point of view. You suspect you'd revert to habit anyway, and write in the second person, that paradoxical perspective that evokes intimacy and detachment—the self and the other; the individual and the communal—all at once. Or you could write under another name. This would also honour your belief that a story is its *own* thing—a worded artefact whose power and meaning derives only from its interaction with the mind of the reader.

You recoil from these permissive lines of reasoning. No! I cannot write *this* story, you think. I cannot pick over the corpse of a *real* dead baby. I won't. I can't.

Except that, of course, you can.

You can do whatever the hell you want.

Suddenly, you are asking him, Do you ever feel that there is a wall between you and others? Do you ever feel like there is a *wall* between you—your self—and others?

Ivan doesn't reply. Won't look at you. He seems annoyed—or embarrassed. But why? Because he doesn't understand? Or because he understands exactly what you mean, but are refusing to admit?

I don't feel anything properly—I don't feel anything.

I don't understand anything properly—I don't understand anything.

I am watching everything, and everything is like a story: and then this happened, and then this happened, and then this happened. And that's all there ever is.

Is there something wrong with me?

The three of you keep winding through the gums alongside the creek until you are staring up at the waterfall. A torrent of water surges over the huge granite cliff. Spray fills the cutting, dampening your skin and misting the dog's black fur with a delicate cloak of translucent, twinkling white.

How many thousands of years has this waterfall been here, just as it is, without change? Such a predictable question (one of those big questions you'd never tackle head-on in your work) yet it is something that you ponder all the time because this—*this here*—is the only perspective you give a damn about: the stunning, complex, timeless, amoral, utterly savage *indifference* of nature.

Staring up at that granite cliff, you finally understand something that has shaped your entire life—something which you have never, yet, pinned down with words. You've always been repelled by the so-called love of others. You've always been repelled by others' so-called desire. You only love things that cannot love you back. That's it. You only love things that do not coerce reciprocation. Yes, it's places that you love—and animals— because places and animals *let you be*.

Fuck it. Write what you want to write.

Write what you need to write.

Stories belong to everyone—and words, after all, are the only human place you've ever felt at home in.

II

It's the morning after. Last night, neither asleep nor awake, you couldn't tell if you were thinking or dreaming. Either way, your mind raced through the hours, so it's no wonder that the slow-burn headache you went to bed with has morphed into a roaring migraine. Even in the dark omnipresence of this familiar old pain, you sense the nature of the conversation Ivan is having in the kitchen. Again, that hardness in his voice. Again, the abrupt staccato-rhythm of bad news.

But how can there be more bad news? Hasn't the worst happened?

You drag yourself out of bed, your head smashing into itself at every turn. Go to the kitchen. Watch him end the call and slide the phone into his pocket.

He stares at you. He is very pale. He says, It came out this morning.

The lump in your throat that began to grow yesterday—that wretched lump of materialising memory—gains another immutable layer of understanding. A whoosh of dizziness rushes up from your feet, turning your legs to water. You cover your mouth. A flutter of panic bursts in you.

What do you mean "it came out"? I thought . . . I thought it was born yesterday? Why didn't you *tell* me?

I didn't know! he says. I didn't *know*! He makes a strange sound. Coughs. Rubs his hands roughly over his face and then shoves past you, making you stumble.

The room tips and turns. Your head bangs into itself—bang, bang, bang. You have to stop for a moment to regain your balance.

You follow him to his study. He stands next to his desk where another day's work awaits him. You stare at his back from the doorway. Just like yesterday, everything about him slumps. He looks desolate—utterly and completely alone.

Pure blinding rage at his mother flashes through you. That woman with her endless babbling. That stupid babbling woman with her endless bloody words but never—never ever—words about *anything* that matters! Why didn't she make it *clear*?! Didn't she *care* that her daughter-in-law had a dead baby inside her? Or did she only care that her grandson—*her* grandson— was dead? Surely not. Surely not. Don't be cruel. Don't judge. Don't judge the stupid bitch ... but you are remembering what she said the first time you spoke to her on the phone, yesterday morning: "It's so unfair, to have come so far. To have come so close." What exactly had she meant? So unfair—for whom? To have come so close—to what? You assumed, then, that she meant Mel and Stefan and their dead-ended pregnancy, but perhaps she was referring to herself. To the refugee who has lost her own mother and father, her home, her language, her profession. To the soon-to-be-grandma who, instead of finally winning a life-affirming vindication that all of her hard choices had been for the best, had simply added another loss to the endless list of losses she drags around with her. She must feel cursed. Perhaps she is.

Ivan? *Ivan!*

He ignores you.

You could go to him—should you go to him?—but your anger is lassoing him in now too. Why didn't he ask more questions? (Why didn't *you*?)

You're wobbly all over. You stumble back to your bedroom. Your head thunders, amplifying yesterday's slow-burn nausea into persistent waves of sickness.

You close the curtains, turn off the lights, take some pills from your bedside drawer and lie down. You know what you're in for. Hours in bed. Hours of agony. Hours of vomiting, too, if you're unlucky.

You focus on breathing slowly and deeply, trying to force calm upon your nervous system's hyperactivity so that you can keep the pills in your stomach long enough for them to be absorbed. You breathe, and try to piece together what has happened from the second-hand scraps of barely comprehended information you've been given these past twenty-four hours. For a moment, you're grateful for the macabre puzzle of it all: it's a compelling distraction, and you know from experience that distraction is one of pain's most powerful enemies.

So, this is the new picture—the revised story. Mel woke up yesterday morning and knew that something was wrong. Her baby wasn't moving. She and Stefan went to the hospital and found out that their baby was dead. That's what you got wrong. That's what neither you nor Ivan understood:

the baby had died, but had not been born. The baby had died, *but had not been born.*

You'd both thought, yesterday, that she'd been through it. You'd both thought, yesterday, that the worst had happened. But no, all day, yesterday, Mel was trapped in the hospital with a dead baby trapped inside her. All day, yesterday—while you ate and worked and walked and pontificated on writing and nature, and then had dinner and watched TV—Mel was trapped in the hospital with a dead baby trapped inside her, surrounded by people who were watching and waiting for "it" to "come out."

"Come out"?! What does that benign little phrase even *mean*?

You are glad, now, that you're not at the hospital spectating her torture. You are certain now—no matter your own motives—that that would be a wrong thing.

Migraines create their own time and consciousness, so you don't know if minutes or hours have passed when you hear him on the phone again. You struggle out of bed and return to his study. He looks up at you, taps his head, his brows raised, silently asking how your headache is. The drugs have blunted the pain a little. You nod and shrug and move in closer, standing next to him where he sits at his desk. Like yesterday, he puts the phone on speaker and lays it on the polished wooden surface. Unlike yesterday, he puts his arm around your waist and pulls you close. You put your hand on his shoulder and he leans his head against your stomach.

Petra is working on her narrative again.

Very early this morning, the two sets of grandparents were told to wait outside a room on another floor of the hospital. They weren't allowed to see their children. They could not hear anything at first, but soon muffled sounds leaked through the air vents and under the closed door, getting louder and louder. A woman saying: "Push, Push, Push." A man saying, "Good girl, good girl, good girl." Someone screaming: "Get it out of me. Get it out of me. Get it out of me."

For once, you're grateful for the compulsive story-telling of Petra—for how she simply reports these horrifying details rather than elaborates upon them. On she goes, her matter-of-fact tone hardly changing when she says, I thought he would come out alive. When we were waiting, I just *knew* he would be ok. She pauses. Then she describes meeting her dead grandson in another part of the hospital, in a tiny room—a specially made room—attached to his mother's.

She says, He looked lovely! He was wrapped up in a cotton blanket. A yellow blanket. Very soft. She pauses, perhaps hearing—as you are—the echo of her words from yesterday: "They made me a special blanket ... a special blanket, to wrap him in ... a blanket, to hold him in."

She says, I thought he was asleep. He looked like he was sleeping. His hair stuck out everywhere—so thick and black! We wanted to see it properly. But, but we weren't allowed to touch his little cap, because ...

She stops. Starts again. Says, Such a big baby!

You cannot tell if her tone is one of pride or horror. She makes him sound monstrous—because he was monstrous—which is why he's dead.

On she goes, describing his tiny ears and the shape of his closed eyes

45

and little nose and pretty mouth—the shape of his chubby cheeks and his strong little chin and the incredible silkiness of his flawless skin. Though she never describes Aleks' reaction (or her own, for that matter), she details how, when Mel's father finally saw his grandson, he started bawling and could not stop. She says, He *completely* lost control. She describes how his wife—the other mother—marched him straight into the corridor. Describes how, as she escorted him away, Mel's younger sister appeared—having just arrived from the airport—and, seeing her father cry for the first time in her entire life, took fright and started crying too. Mel's mother didn't flinch or fuss. She just whisked them both down the hall. Mother and daughter soon returned to Mel's room—hand-in-hand, recomposed—but the father seems to have disappeared.

Petra keeps noting how *calm* Mel's mother is. Even when they all sat and listened to her daughter screaming through the air vents. Even when she saw her—their—dead grandson, even *then* this other mother knew what to do. She didn't cry or shake or anything like that. She just kissed and stroked his sweet little face and chatted to him as if it were the most natural thing in the world. She's so *calm*, Petra says again. So *calm*, so *natural*.

You realise then that, after all, Petra is telling you exactly how she herself feels: panicked, unnatural, weepy, shaky, speechless. You realise she has been studying this other mother for clues on to how to behave, apparently oblivious to the possibility that what looks like calmness might be numbness, and that what looks like naturalness might just be the behaviour of a woman running on autopilot—enacting a feminine, maternal, wifely script that she has spent her entire life absorbing and practising.

Now Petra is describing every single person that has come into Mel's room this morning. (You realise it is lunchtime. You've been asleep for hours.) Family, friends, doctors, nurses, counsellors, cleaners. She describes—as if it were an everyday thing—how Mel spent the morning propped up on a huge cloud of pillows, flying high on all sorts of drugs, chatting and laughing, then crumpling and crying. She details every single meal that the staff have brought in—all "terrible"—and describes how an army of women from her own family have started to arrive, filling up the room's little fridge with plates from home.

You feel a pulse of rage—the flaring of old anxieties. You know those women. You spent the first decade of your life with Ivan being dominated and bullied by their so-called "care": feeding people (who don't want fed), advising people (who don't want advice), helping people (who don't want help). Those grasping women who are nobody unless they are somebody's mother or daughter or wife or sister or aunt. Those desperate women who dress their hunger for attention and power and control as virtue—as love! How *dare* they impose at such a time! Is nothing on this planet ever private? Is nothing ever—automatically, without a bloody *fight*—free from intrusion and spectation?

You picture your own grandmother giving birth, alone. Baptising her baby, alone. Watching it die, alone, and then going home to a world that refused to acknowledge what had happened. You picture her, sixty years after that event, compulsively seeking witness, judgement, absolution.

Both scenarios—your grandmother's and Mel's—*both* situations seem so cruel, so extreme, so completely and utterly isolating.

Now Petra is saying things like, Life goes on. Of course, this is true—for you, and Ivan, and probably for her, too. But will it be true for Mel and Stefan? *Can* their lives "go on" after what has happened to them?

Petra's not finished. She says, Next time they'll be more careful. Next time they'll do the tests. Get it cut out earlier.

Your body braces and your heart races and your face floods with heat. What is Mel? A breeding sow? A hunk of meat? And which "they" should "be more careful"? Is it the parents' fault their baby died? How can anyone be thinking of "next time" already?

If you don't know the right words, Petra, *shut up, shut up, shut up*.

Abruptly, you step back from Ivan and leave the room. You sit on your bed. Your headache is worsening again. You lean over to get more drugs from your bedside drawer, but a surge of nausea sends you stumbling to the toilet.

You wake up on the floor. You are lying on your side, staring at the wall. You feel so relaxed—as if you're in a dream. It takes you a moment to work out where you are. Vaguely, you realise your migraine and nausea are gone. Vaguely, you realise you are warm and damp—you've wet yourself. Then a rushing sound fills your head—rushing, as loud as a train.

Something touches your shoulder. You turn your head slightly. It's Ivan—Ivan crouching over you, shaking you. He looks scared.

He says, You blacked out. I heard you fall. You've hit your face on the tiles.

You try to respond to him, but you can't talk. (*If you don't know the right words, shut up, shut up, shut up.*)

He reaches for a towel. Mops up your mess. Finds another towel, dampens it. You watch it blotch with red as he gently presses it into your nose. It's bleeding a little, he says. Don't worry. Slowly, he stands you up, undresses you, kicks your pyjamas to the corner, dries you properly and walks you to the bedroom. He lays you back in bed, naked, and tucks you in tight. You're shivering. He disappears and comes back with a blanket. He sits on the bed next to you and strokes your face. He just sits there, patting you, until your shivering stops and the rushing sound fades and you are able to talk again. You manage to speak, to apologise.

He shakes his head. Tucks you in tighter. Don't be silly, he says. Nothing to be sorry about. He keeps stroking your face—looking just as worried as you feel—because, though it's not the first time you've keeled over like this, it is the first time you've wet yourself and the first time you've been deafened by a storm of blood. What does it mean? Is there something wrong with you?

Weeks after this, you will go to see your doctor in the city and you will tell her about this weird faint. The doctor will ask you for all the details: what, where, when. You will be surprised by your sudden inability to speak, until you realise that it is the first time you've told anyone about what happened. You'll realise that you haven't said the story aloud yet. That you've only recited versions of the story to yourself, inside your head. That, though it is weeks after the baby was due, none of your own friends or family know that he is, in fact, long dead.

In a shaking voice, you will finally manage to say, My partner's brother's ... my sister-in-law ... lost her baby. Her baby died just before she was meant to give birth.

Typing with one finger, and without looking away from her screen, the doctor will pass you a box of tissues.

You will dab your eyes, but your unexpected tears will keep coming, and this will utterly bewilder you. Why am I crying *now*? you'll think. I didn't cry when it happened. I didn't *care* when it happened—or afterwards. None of it had anything to *do* with me. But even as you think this, you will hear yourself say, for the first time, Our nephew ... and you won't be able to say anything more. Instead, you will humiliate yourself with uncontrollable, ugly sobs.

Coolly, the doctor will continue to type and look at her screen and will suggest the connection that, of course, will be so stupidly obvious. (*Most of your goddamn life is obvious.*) Your faint and migraine most likely resulted from shock, from stress, from grief. And so, after all, it will appear that you *did* feel something when it happened. You *did* care, somehow. Your body— if not your mind—fully comprehended the terrible suffering of other human animals.

Maybe that was—that is—the most that anyone can ever hope for. Maybe that's *everything*.

Blurry-eyed, you will watch the doctor type the word "stillborn" into your file. She will record it so casually—as if it is as common as the flu—and you'll wonder, How often does this happen? How common *is* it?

Stillborn.

You've always known this word, but this doctor will be the first person to associate it directly with your nephew. You'll realise, then, that no one in Ivan's family has used that word at all. Why not? In your teary mess, you'll clutch at it like a life raft, momentarily buoyed by its apt and gentle poetry: the baby *was* stillborn because, though he died in the home of his mother, he was *still* hers and he was *still* to be born. He was born still—not moving—but he was also still in the most subtle, temporal sense of that word, in how he became a continuity linking one time to another: a dream from the past that shaped a reality in the present; a reality in the present that seared a scar onto the future.

After your appointment, you'll go to catch the train. It's a long trip home from the city, through wide open spaces, and you'll be glad for this after your embarrassment in the doctor's stuffy office. You'll plonk down in a corner of the carriage and flick through a newspaper that someone has left on the seat beside you. You'll read the obituaries—as you always do—enjoying the poignant pull of each cliché-filled notice. You'll calculate the ages of the dead, and work out who is the most popular corpse for the day—that is, who has the longest or most eloquent or most numerous messages—and you'll almost read right over this tiny line: "For Ava. Born Sleeping." This notice will have no birth date, or death date—no narrative arc. You'll immediately recognise it as another life-death. You will stare at it and realise,

This—this *here*—is the world's shortest story. You'll read it again, then again, and the hot wild tears from the doctor's office will rush up in you. You'll use the newspaper to shield your face from the other passengers, focusing on the new phrase as you try to get a grip on yourself. Born sleeping. A phrase that you'll never have heard before that train ride. Born sleeping. A phrase that you'd never have noticed—or understood—before that moment.

What are the chances, you'll think, that I'd come across this phrase right now—right after the doctor reminds me that the common and correct word to describe what's happened is "stillborn"? If this were a story, you'll think, this newspaper and this obituary—placed as they are—would read as too convenient a coincidence, as too crude and obvious a literary device and, therefore, as a gross authorial intervention into the text. Yet, you'll think, this coincidence *is* the reality. What is a writer meant to do when facts *are* "stranger than fiction"? How many stories, you'll think, have I not written—or destroyed through endless excisions—because the realities that shaped them seemed implausible? How on earth can fiction demand more realism than reality itself?!

You once saw a fox trot up to a lamb that was sunbathing under a tree. The fox stopped, picked up an apple that had fallen to the ground, and then went on his way, the bright red fruit gleaming in his jaws. You have tried to insert this scene into your stories many times, not because it meant anything, but because it was beautiful to watch (in the most visual, aesthetic sense of that word), and because, quite simply, *it happened*. Each of your attempts failed, however, with the scene somehow forcing an unwelcome symbolic—almost biblical—dimension onto your texts. In other words, this incident seemed doomed to become a metaphor on the page: something that stood in for something else; something abstract, instead of something concrete and real. Is this a fault in how we write, you've wondered, with each disaster. Or is this a fault in how we read? The prof was right. *Most of your goddamn life is obvious.* Things are almost always exactly, and only, what they appear to be and there's something wrong with a literary realism that denies the fact that sometimes foxes choose apples over lambs.

On that future train ride, you will reflect upon all of this as you try to regain your composure. You will then put down the paper, stare out the window, and turn the two phrases over in your mind. Stillborn. Born Sleeping. Stillborn. Born Sleeping. You will feel the texture and weight of them. You will feel the tenderness and compassion at the core of each of them, though it will be the second phrase that will resonate with you the most—for, didn't everyone say how, even when they saw your nephew, they couldn't believe he was dead? Didn't everyone say that he looked just like any other newborn, asleep in its crib? Didn't everyone say that, despite knowing what they knew, they were sure he'd awaken? And do they still? you'll wonder. Do they still think he'll wake up? For how *can* you believe that someone is dead if you've never seen them alive?

But all of this—the meaning-making time-travel of memory and narrative—lies in your future. Right now, you are tucked into bed after blacking out and wetting yourself and feeling a devastation of blood riot within you. You are lying in bed, scared for your health and nervous about what you and Ivan are meant to do, now that you know what the worst of it was— now that you know the worst of it is, finally, over.

III

The next morning, Petra says you can visit.

You don't know what to wear. You know no one will notice or care about how you look, but it takes you over an hour to choose something anyway. In the end, you wear your most expensive and plainest clothes: a dark green, classically-cut dress and black flats. You apply understated makeup, carefully masking the slight bruising around your nose from yesterday's fall. You are grotesquely "smart casual." You feel helpless—completely inadequate to this task though you know that being adequate to this task would be the most grotesque and unnatural thing of all.

Ivan appears, looking clean and neat and classy.

You simultaneously compliment each other. Laugh. You might as well be getting dressed up for a night out.

It's a long drive to the city. You listen to the radio and chat about everything except the reason you're driving, and it's only once you reach the city's suburban fringe that you begin to feel anxious. You start looking for a florist, though you're not sure if you're meant to buy flowers for such an occasion. Flowers are for births, deaths, illnesses, achievements. Well, haven't Mel and Stefan experienced all of these things in the past few days?

Ivan shrugs, annoyed. Why get them anything? he says. There's nothing that can help. They won't care.

You wonder if he's being cheap—and you wonder at your own motives. You think of all the women from his family who have brought in food and toiletries and magazines. Are you buying something because you fear *their* judgement? Or are you buying flowers out of guilt—guilt at being glad that this horrible thing hasn't happened to *you*? Guilt that you've been more fascinated—than aggrieved—by Mel and Stefan's loss?

You finally spot a florist. Ivan refuses to come in, so you leave him in the car and go by yourself. It's a tiny corner shop, with huge folded-back doors. Plastic buckets of bouquets are attached to every inner and outer surface, climbing all the way up to the ceiling: suburban epiphytes. The florist comes out from the back. He is tall and skinny, with olive skin and thick black curls. He nods and says hello with a European accent that you can't quite place.

Thankfully, he gets busy behind the counter and leaves you in peace.

You have no idea what to choose. Blue flowers? Is there such a thing? What about yellow, that gender-neutral colour that so many people prefer for baby-gifts? . . . but there is no baby.

You finally settle on white. You know that, in China, white has everything to do with death and funerals, and your mother once described to you a tradition in the remote isles of Scotland, where pregnant women would carefully sew their own white death shrouds along with the clothes they made for their yet-to-be-born babies. They'd lay their shrouds out, ready, just before giving birth. They did this simply as a matter of course. Over there, unlike here, the closeness of death to birth was openly acknowledged—and accepted. Yes, white flowers make the most sense, if anything makes sense.

You choose peonies. You carefully extract one bunch, and then another from the bucket. Up close, they are a rich buttery cream. A warm white. Lovely. And they're huge, sumptuous, triumphant, a ridiculous display of nature's random artistry and excess. You take them to the counter. The florist nods at your choice. You feel stupidly relieved. He gestures at the reels of ribbon lined up on a dowel attached to the wall. He seems to sense that you don't want to—can't—chitty chat. You study the satin rainbow. There are blue ribbons, of course, but seeing them makes you realise how weird it would be to give them something blue. Another flush of relief goes through you—as if you've avoided a misstep. You point to the roll of earthy twine at the side of the counter. Again, the florist nods with approval.

An elderly lady wanders in as he carefully snips open each bunch, combines them together, then wraps them in white tissue and brown paper. He's taking his time, taking great care. As you wait, you watch the woman lug her big old shopping cart around. The cart, and her huge jacket, keep knocking into things, making her mutter. She wanders slowly, touching this and that, while constantly looking over at you and the florist. Once or twice, he stops in his work and glares at her. She smiles sweetly and keeps wandering. All of a sudden, he barks at her in Italian. She reels back, her palms up in a parody of self-defence. He repeats the same words, jabbing his finger with each syllable, and then points to the street. *Out*, he says. The woman whispers something to herself, then huffs and puffs towards the door, banging her cart, exaggerating her every movement and nearly knocking over the buckets of flowers that line the doorway.

The florist resumes his careful wrapping. Sad but true, he says. The old ones are the worst. That lady? She is always here, trying to steal things. She knows *I* will get in trouble if I touch her—try to stop her. The old ones—and the mamas with their prams—they are *terrible*. He shakes his head, tying the twine into multiple bows. *People*, he mutters, people are always the very worst or the very best of things, no?

You nod dumbly, wondering if you are the very worst or the very best of things.

He hands you the flowers. As you turn to leave, he gently lays his fingertips on your forearm. He locks his eyes with yours—forcing you to look directly into their clear, pale green—and he says: I am very sorry for your loss, *bella*.

You look away. You look down at the flowers crooked in your arm, held exactly as you'd hold a baby. Is that what he's noticed? Of course not. He's just seen thousands of people at the happiest and saddest times of their life. It's his job, after all, to help people say something where words can only fail.

Back at the car, you open the rear door and lay the flowers carefully on the seat. Ivan turns. He glares at you, then glares at the bouquet. What is his problem? Did you spend too much money—or did you get the wrong thing? Or is it, maybe, that he just wants to get everything over with and you're holding him up? Is that why he thinks you wanted to buy flowers—to postpone the inevitable? Is it true? Well, yes. It is true. You'd postpone what lies ahead of you forever if you could.

You remember the tone of Petra's voice when she whispered, "What do I say to them?" She'd sounded so frightened, and that's exactly how you feel right now. Frightened. Scared. Sick with nerves. You know that you're about to perform inadequately in yet another scene from the eternal, coercive pantomime of Family. (As if you could ever show Mel and Stefan that you care and understand! You don't care! You will never understand!) But your fear has also been stirred by the florist. Not from what he said, or did—but from what he noticed. He clearly saw what you yourself can hardly see. He clearly saw what you thought was hidden deep within you. His noticing has shown you that, though this baby is dead, he still lives—somehow—in the world. Of course, you think. Of course he lives. Because, even if you *could* hide a pregnancy, or the death of a baby, you cannot hide—or kill—a ghost.

As Ivan drives to the hospital, the streets get busier and busier. You look at the thousands of ordinary people milling about their ordinary lives and you wonder how many of them are also trailed by ghosts? How many of them are broken, but acting whole? How many of them are in pain right now—and is their pain ever noticed or salved by others? And what about you? You've had pain too. You've had losses ... but surely yours are miniscule compared to Mel's and Stefan's. Surely your losses are nothing compared to theirs—or Petra's. Surely such things are relative?

Your mother used to teach migrants English. She'd recount the savage competition between a certain kind of student they had—a competition she called "The Pain Game." She'd make a joke of it, though she'd get furious at the way students, who'd each been through so much themselves, nevertheless needed to put each other down. "There is no realm of experience," she'd say, "that is free from status anxiety." Then she'd imitate her students, to make you laugh—and to make her point.

"You lost your home? I lost my arm!"

"You lost your arm? I lost my wife!"

"You lost your wife? I lost my child!"

"You lost your child? I lost my whole family!"

"You lost your family? I lost my home, my family, my village, my country *and* both of my legs!"

She'd "jokingly" tell them that they were making her "lose her mind" but later, privately, she'd find and console whomever had had their grief trivialised by their classmates. She knew there was nothing "relative" about suffering. Watching them taught her that pain is pain, and it can grow to fill whatever space is made available to it in a mind, a body, a family, a home, a nation, a history. She said that this made perfect sense to her. It reminded her of how, when she was pregnant with her second child, she feared that she wouldn't—no, *couldn't*—love it. She already loved her first child so much—surely she had no more love left to give?! But her love didn't halve with her second child: instead—impossibly!—it doubled. Then it tripled with the third. And quadrupled with the fourth. It's hardly surprising then, that pain—which is love's child—should behave in just the same way. "Both are unique elements," she'd said. "Both can grow and grow and grow—if you let them."

You gaze at the people in the street. Busy, busy, busy. Ordinary, ordinary, ordinary. What have they seen? What do they know? What do they feel? Are they broken? Whole? Are they—can they, must we—be both at once?

Covertly, you glimpse Ivan's face as he parks the car. You cannot read it. Even after all these years he often seems as foreign and inscrutable, to you, as any stranger. You get out of the car. You open the back door and carefully lift the flowers from the seat. Ivan comes around and takes them from you, gripping them by their bound stems and holding them in front of his body like a weapon. They're just right, he says, his light tone denying his earlier irritation and the way his free hand roughly clutches for yours.

As you walk, you squeeze his hand. He squeezes yours back. You squeeze his again, harder, and he does the same. You keep playing this silly old game as you approach the huge building that straddles the end of the road. It's a concrete monolith, squatting over two city blocks—a prime example of Cold War, brutalist architecture. A multilevel walkway joins the two buildings over the road's heaving chaos of traffic. Suddenly, a siren wails and—without hesitation—the chaos instantly slows to a stop as hundreds of hassled strangers *(... the very best ...)* think with one mind, working together to clear a path so that some unknown person, somewhere, can get the help they desperately need. The ambulance pulls out from the belly of the hospital, winds slowly through the awkward clearway, then screams off into the distance. The traffic surges on.

You keep walking. With each squeeze of—and from—Ivan's hand, another pulse of savage gladness assaults you, the same vicious gratitude that overwhelmed you when you first heard the terrible news.

Thank God it's them and not us (... *the very worst* ...).

Thank God it's *them*, not *us* (... *the very worst* ...).

May we always be the lucky ones. May the only ghosts that shadow us be the ghosts of strangers.

The hospital is like an airport inside: sterile, shiny, clean, busy and chock full of shops. Just like an airport, it's a paradoxical space: completely impersonal, yet fraught with feeling.

Ivan seems to know where he's going. You follow him down corridors and through cafeterias and past shops till you are in an elevator zooming upwards. Neither of you says anything. In the elevator's mirrored walls Ivan's face looks normal. So does yours—despite the panic fluttering at your edges. You feel weak in your legs, and you're worried that you're going to faint and wet yourself again. How ridiculously *Austenesque*, you think. How melodramatic the body can be!

You step out of the elevator into a fluro-lit passage. Ivan leads you down endless corridors until—too quickly—you're standing before one of many identical doors. Ivan knocks.

There is no sound other than your and Ivan's breathing, and the rustling of the paper-wrapped flowers as he moves them from one hand to another.

He knocks again—louder. The door swings open.

It's the reality—not the idea of the reality.

It's the person—not the idea of the person.

It's Stefan.

He looks normal—sort of.

Normal, but dishevelled and pale and stubbly. Though his face is puffy and ruddy, his eyes look very clear and very bright.

You step forward and hug him in the doorway. You stand back.

Ivan steps forward and hugs his brother.

Then you all move into the room.

Where is she? someone asks.

She's in the bathroom, Stefan says, then he makes a lame joke about something.

You all laugh. You are all making dumb jokes and laughing. Stefan points things out in the room, as if giving you a tour: the big hospital bed (he demonstrates with a remote control how it can be tilted up and down in different places, like a caterpillar); an armchair; a table; a TV mounted high on the wall (turned on, muted); some extra chairs stacked in a corner; the door to the bathroom; a tiny kitchenette with a kettle and fridge. There is another door that Stefan ignores. You realise it must lead to the viewing-room that Petra spoke of. Stefan jokes about all the food stuffed into the fridge by his aunties. And that's my bed, he says, pointing to a flimsy pull-out folded up in the corner. Like camping, he says.

As you stand, waiting, you look around and realise that this is an exceptionally private and well-equipped room—not what anyone would expect in a public hospital. Clearly, when your baby dies, you get extra special treatment. (The sick, cynical absurdity of this instantly hits you—for, if Mel and Stefan had had "extra special treatment" while she was pregnant, mightn't their baby have lived?) You wonder if all the other rooms lining the corridor are like this. Are they all occupied, right now, with the parents of dead babies? How often does this happen?

Despite this being a "good" room, it feels claustrophobic. It is windowless. It feels like the internal cabin of a ship: hot and dark and damp. And it smells strange. There is something sickly sweet behind the immediate, incongruent smells of disinfectant and food.

Stefan points to a clutter of machines next to the bed. He explains that Mel has been pumping milk since yesterday—milk for other babies. You learn that there is a milk bank—as well as a blood bank—in this hospital.

You've all run out of things to say. You stand, and wait, and look at everything except each other until—thank goodness—a door opens softly.

There she is. Here she is.

It's the reality—not the idea of the reality.

It's the person—not the idea of the person.

It's Mel.

For a moment, she just blinks at you and Ivan, her eyes adjusting to the dimness of the bedroom after the fluorescent lights of the bathroom.

Like Stefan, she looks the same—sort of.

Like Stefan, she looks familiar—sort of.

She is definitely the same person you saw a week or so ago, except that she's not made up and dressed up and strutting. Instead, she's wearing a pretty floral nightie: it looks brand new. Her hair is brushed and pulled back into a tight ponytail. She looks neat and tidy, but is sallow-skinned and there are caverns under her swollen, blood-shot, red-rimmed eyes. And—this is what you did not expect; this is what confuses you, for a second—she still looks pregnant.

How little you know about any of this. How little you know about anything—about everything. (Remember: you know nothing, nothing, nothing.)

You stare at her from across the room. You are staring at each other, smiling. You are two animals—assessing each other, as if for the very first time. You are staring and smiling at this smiling girl, this smiling woman, who is all fashion and Facebook, dresses and drinking, baby showers and wedding planning. All brittle composure and sharp self-absorption. This woman who always has her painted, glittered face on. This woman, who—more than anyone you know—so carefully constructs a wall between herself and the world.

She looks away for a second. She looks at her hand, at her phone, which is in its usual hot pink case. She swipes the screen, as if checking the time. When she looks up again, her face is folding, crumpling, and she is crying.

In the same second, you and Ivan step towards her—he the brother and you the sister. In this one second, you are—all of you, without question—brothers and sisters.

Together, somehow, you and Ivan hug her, hold her. Both of you are rubbing her back and her arms and her sides—rubbing her briskly as if she is cold and you are trying to warm her up. She feels so incredibly *solid*. It reassures you, how solid she feels, as if some suppressed, terrified part of your mind feared that you'd misunderstood everything—that it was *she* who had died—it was *she* who'd turned into a ghost.

She yelps. Ivan has stepped on her toe! She laughs. Everyone laughs. She jokes, Haven't I been through enough, Ivan?! Then she starts crying again. Then she is laughing. She says, I'm sorry. She says, It's just when I see people—when I *see* people for the first time since . . . I just can't *help* this. She gestures at her face. She shakes her head, wipes her eyes, and walks over to the bed. She walks awkwardly. Stefan helps her. You can see how every part of her hurts—how she has become a body-sized wound. You and Ivan turn away and get busy unstacking two plastic chairs, which you place at the foot of the bed.

Stefan sits on a chair next to Mel, holding her hand. For a moment, the room is completely silent. Then Ivan leans around to inspect the fridge, making everyone laugh at his notorious appetite. He piles up a plate with pastries as Stefan starts to recount the events of the past few days. He chats about who's come and gone. Even when he shrugs and says, Lots of tears, lots of hugs, his tone doesn't change. He is matter-of-fact. He is doing exactly what Petra does: he has already created a story, fattened up with details about nothing that matters. He already has a story, and he's sticking to it—staying safe within it. You watch him, and you listen to him, and you realise that, since Mel came out of the bathroom, he hasn't taken his eyes off her. Though he is chatting to you and Ivan, he is staring at her—staring at her, non-stop, with his strangely bright eyes. Now you can see what's changed in him. Something subtle, but fundamental. He is no longer just her husband. He is her guardian. He is her protector in the most primitive sense of the word. He has seen her suffer as no one should suffer—he suffers for that—and he will never let anything on this planet hurt her again.

After a while, Mel begins to chat too. Already, she almost sounds like her usual self. Already, she is resembling the girl you saw last week. Already, her carefully constructed exterior is pushing itself to the surface. Again—and you cannot believe this—you are *repelled* by it. Stop it! you say to yourself. *Stop it!* But even as you scold yourself, it is relief—not self-disgust—that overwhelms you as you recognise your familiar old reaction to her. Yes, you think. *There* she is. Maybe she's still in there. Maybe she'll be ok. Because you want her back. You want that shallow self-centred woman back. And Stefan—who is chatting away while staring at Mel like a psychopath—you want *him* back too. You want him to bring out his phone and play games on it while Ivan tries to talk to him. You want him to be as abrupt and rude and self-absorbed as he was just last week.

Mel begins to tell the story of the labour. How did this start? Did you ask her? Have other visitors asked her about it—making her assume that you want to hear the details too? Or does she need to talk about it so that she—like Petra and Stefan—can contain the horror with words before the thoughts and feelings and images take on lives of their own?

You look at Ivan. He seems utterly unphased by the disturbing contrast of Mel's gruesome recount and her ordinary voice. He seems utterly unaffected by the pervasive, sickly sweet smell in the hot steamy room. He just sits next to you, nodding away and stuffing his face as if he is watching a movie in a cinema.

On she goes, methodically, calmly, casually.

You steady yourself. You breathe deeply. You feel the lump in your throat—that stray tooth of memory—calcifying each new layer of detail onto the others. You swallow. Try not to retch.

It was such a big baby, she says. The size of a *three month old*. That's why it died. They were meant to induce me. But they didn't. That's why it died. It was like pushing out a *rock*! It went on for hours and hours. First its head got stuck. Then its shoulders. Then its stomach. The doctor was slamming all his weight down on my belly. He was, like, *throwing* himself on me as I pushed and they pulled. I had to wait ages for an epidural—because it was *Sunday*. Then the shot didn't work properly. They had to roll me on my side till I lost feeling in both legs. Then, my feet swelled up like footballs! From the penicillin. Turns out I'm *allergic*! She laughs. I mean, for *fuck's* sake! She sobs. Pauses. Regains control. Keeps chatting.

You sit tight, trying to fight the nausea and dizziness that's spinning through you. You are nodding and smiling at her, though—thankfully, awfully—she is not looking at you. In fact, you realise, for the whole time that she has been talking, she's been staring up and over your head at the muted TV.

God, she says, it fucking *hurt*. I thought I was going to die. Like, *literally*, she says. I thought I was dying. Now, I'm totally *fucked* from the waist down! She laughs, then says she's had to show her vagina to so many strangers. Says how people just walk in, and look, without hardly saying anything to her. For all I know they could be cleaners, she says. Or people off the street—preggo perves! She laughs—so you all laugh—but fury flares in you. At who? You don't know, but you call them They. Why did They make her go through this? Why couldn't They have just knocked her unconscious, and cut the thing out of her? Why force a woman to give birth to something that's dead? And you glimpse what you've never seen—or valued—before.

Women *give* birth to their children. Birthing is a mother's *gift* to her child. Birthing is a gift of pure directional energy, a force—the life force—that propels each tiny soul into the world of the future. So how do you give birth to a dead thing?

As if hearing your thoughts, Mel says, If it was alive it would have helped me. Babies *help* themselves get born. If they are dead, she says, they cannot help.

Then she says, I was screaming: Get it out of me. Get it out of me. Get it out of me.

Then she describes how they shoved the steel forceps all the way into her, jerking out the corpse of her son with bits and pieces of her own flesh, stage by stuck stage.

The dizziness swings through you again as you wonder, How do people survive such things? How does the body—let alone the mind—recover from such things? You know the answer. It doesn't. Survival and recovery are not the same—are they? Didn't Mel just use exactly the same words as your friend—the friend whose labour trauma has become a source of irritation and boredom to everyone around her? "I thought I was dying." How many women walk around with these very words echoing forever within them?

Mel says, You know, babies die like this *all* the time. She shrugs. I didn't know that, she says. I should have known that.

Shut up, you're thinking, just *shut up*, but you can see them, feel them—all these men and women who are in agony while the world just goes about its business outside, ignorant, indifferent. You remember how the hospital seemed to hulk across the city blocks as you and Ivan walked towards it less than an hour ago. It looked more like a fort—or a prison—than a hospital. *That's* what this room feels like—less a cabin in the gut of a ship, than a cell in the steel and concrete maze of a jail. And that's what it is, isn't it? A building designed to quarantine us from the most ordinary realities of all: birth, illness, death. We are the only animals who can think about such things—who can yearn for, and fear, such things—yet we put knowledge of these experiences behind closed doors and into the hands of "experts" who are meant to care for us though they do not even know us.

How are Mel and Stefan meant to step back into the world from this place that seems designed to hide everything they've been through? How will their experience be so different, after all, to what your grandmother suffered? She left her home to have a baby, she came home without a baby, and no one—no one said a word about it.

You ask, Do you have a photo of him? Him. You realise this is the one word that Mel hasn't used. She has only called him "it" and so you're unsure—with her abrupt silence—if you've said the wrong thing or asked to see something that isn't yours to see. Perhaps, except that Stefan leaps up from his chair. Maybe he can't stand hearing these details either. For him, these details are matched with images and an onslaught of sensations—because he was there, he saw all of it. If Mel was trapped on the inside of her experience, he was trapped on the outside, seeing everything but unable to stop it, end it, fix it.

He rifles about near his camp bed and then, with a shaking hand, gives you a white envelope.

And here he is.

The reality—not the idea of the reality.

The person—not the idea of the person.

Him—not it.

First, a black and white photo of his little face, close up, side on. He is so neat, so cute—pure perfection, like every new baby. His eyes are closed and he is wrapped up snugly, wearing the little hat that Petra mentioned. Just as she said, there's ridiculously thick black hair sticking out from underneath it, framing his face.

There's a close up of his hands. Huge and chubby—made of dimples.

There are footprints in black ink.

Handprints.

Who took his little dead body and cleaned him, then dipped his hands and feet in ink, and then cleaned him again? Who did this?

Who wrapped him up carefully, tightly, as if to comfort him—keep him safe? Who did this?

Who covered the forceps-wounds and his hacked-up skull with the soft little cap—then carefully pulled his hair down around his face so that people could admire it? Who did this?

Who took these beautiful photos that show who he was—apart from the trauma of what has happened to him? Who did this?

Who are these invisible people doing this invisible work? What do they feel? What do they think? Is it, for them, just a job? For clearly there is a standardised process here—they know exactly what they're doing, because they've done it many times before. How *often* does this happen?

You study each photo again.

You understand, now, that this baby was his very own self.

You understand, now, that he was alive before he was dead.

Your hands are shaking, just as Stefan's were a moment ago. You feel your face quivering. Tears are threatening, but you stop them—quick smart—when you feel Mel and Stefan flinch.

Do others' tears trigger theirs?

Are they embarrassed at having such intimacies forced upon their own?

Or do they just not know what to do with all these tears being shed before—and for—them?

Perhaps it's anger. If you were trapped in this place—in this hell—captive to the needy grief of others, you'd feel angry too.

You manage to say, He's so cute. You manage to say, He's a cute little fatso. They both laugh.

Fatty boomba, Mel says, from her cloud of pillows. Fat little bubba.

You hand the photos to Ivan. He puts down his plate, wipes his hands, takes the photos and, like you, studies them very slowly, very closely, one-by-one. You realise he is following your lead—using the photos to hide his face. You realise he's been eating, all this time, for the very same reason. You realise his face isn't bright and rosy because he's an oblivious, overfed idiot—but because he, like you, is supressing boiling hot tears.

Eventually, he puts the photos carefully back into the envelope and returns them to his brother. They don't look at each other. Ivan sits back in his seat, twists around, and leans down to the fridge to take out another slice of cake. Everyone laughs. He shrugs helplessly, smiling and eating and refusing to raise his hot-cheeked, tearful—tear full—face.

You watch him and, with a wrench, realise that you love him very, very much. How could you ever have doubted this, over the years? This soft-eyed, soft-faced man who—you can see now—feels so many things, so deeply. That savage gratitude assails you again. You are grateful—grateful that it's *not* his son, not your son, that has died. Grateful that you haven't had to endure anything like this, not yet. You recite it—your new refrain—your selfish prayer: May we always be the lucky ones. May we always, *always* be the lucky ones.

Finally, you are interrupted by a gentle knock at the door. A nurse bustles in with Mel and Stefan's dinner. The day has passed, somehow, and it is time for you and Ivan to leave.

As you hug your goodbyes, the room fills with relief. Mel and Stefan have survived another visit. They are only one night away from fleeing the hospital. They are going to a house somewhere far away: her family's old beach shack. Her parents have already been there to cut the grass and spook the snakes. They are going away to be alone with this terribly unexpected aloneness. Stefan mutters something about putting off "facing everyone, explaining everything." It's as if they've done something wrong and they're fleeing the scene of the crime. (*Where's your baby? I left him behind! Where?! In the past, the past, the past.*) You remember Mel's Instagram and Facebook posts. All those images of her beautiful pregnant body and the ultrasounds and the baby shower and the nursery. How crass and boastful they seemed then—and what a reckless temptation of fate they seem like now. Can such things be deleted? Should they? What will she post now? A statement? A refusal to state?

In a few months' time, you and Ivan will witness Mel's solution to this problem of "what to say" to the ever-watching, ever-waiting ether. Three months after her final boastful selfie (a gap of time rendered invisible by the feed's relentless, compressing chronology) she will post a link to an organisation. The words she will attach to her post will be impersonal—and expressed in the strange language of hashtags: #stillbirthresearch #stillbirthawareness #endpreventablestillbirth.

She is a better writer than me, you'll think. She truly knows the power of understatement—the power of showing over telling.

Without making a personal comment, without writing a story (at least, not a story as you know it) Mel will say all that needs to be said. Through her link and her hashtags, she will let everyone know what happened to her and what has happened—and keeps happening—to so many others.

Her post will be a cry of sorrow and a cry for help (#stillbirthfamily #stillbirthmommy #dadsgrievetoo).

It will be a pledge of solidarity (#stillbirthsurvivor).

It will also be a warning—like a sign on a highway—reminding everyone that there are wilds on either side of the road which anyone can veer into at any time (#love, #griefjourney).

But more than anything, her post will be a protest—a roar of anger: #6babiesaday

You and Ivan will read this, and wonder, How can this be—in one of the best healthcare systems in the world? And, if it's so common—how come we never hear of it?

Of course, you'll recognise that Mel's post is both exposing and smashing this taboo (#breakthesilence #stillbirthmatters). You'll see how, unlike your grandmother, Mel will *not* hide her baby's death as if it's a personal shame. (*You cannot hide a pregnancy. You cannot hide a dead baby. You cannot—you must not—hide the presence of such absences.*) With one post, Mel will demand that people stop, pay attention, and talk about what the walls of the public hospital—and the pain of personal grief—keep hidden from them. With one post, Mel will demand that, though she cannot talk about it yet, everyone else must.

But then, a few days after this post, she *will* begin to talk about it—in her own way. She will upload the photo you saw in the hospital. The black and white photo of her baby, taken from side on, showing his perfect little face and his outrageous black hair. Again, she won't write anything other than her says-nothing, says-everything hashtags: #saytheirname #davidnovak #bornsleeping.

It will seem macabre to you, at first, how scores of people will "like" and "share" this post—macabre, until people start posting photos of their own #angelbabies. Then you will recognise how, just like your precious books, the power of social media lies in its capacity to create texts that are both private and public at once. You'll see how, just like your precious books, this medium magically unites the lives and minds of scattered people—friends and strangers—but does so in real-time, and more intensely, more inclusively, more ... *audibly* than books ever can.

Together, you and Ivan will read all of the too-public, too-private messages left for Mel, messages left by people determined to tell her that they hear what she is telling them (without telling them), that some of them (too many of them) have been through it too, that they understand—and are so very, very sorry.

You are driving from the hospital to his parents' house. Visiting them is the next and final scene in this act of your shared story. You know how it will unfold. The kitchen blinds will flicker as you pull into the drive. Petra will open the door. Aleks will appear behind her and peer over her shoulder. Standing there, like that—morphed into silhouettes by the backlit doorway—they will look so anonymous and small that something will clutch sharply inside of you.

You will ignore this feeling—will refuse to look at it, refuse to name it.

You and Ivan will get out of the car. His parents will step forward and hug you. In the warm light cast from the doorway you will see Petra's face tremble. You will feel yours tremble too. For a second, you will just stand there, looking at each other, noticing each other's tears—noticing each other force those same tears back.

Maybe you've misunderstood, all along, what closeness and caring means. Maybe closeness and caring have nothing to do with thoughts or feelings, with liking or loving. Nothing, certainly, to do with words. Maybe closeness and caring are only, in the end, about proximity—proximity and witnessing.

Quickly, briskly, Petra will smile and say, "I'm fine. It's *fine*." She and Aleks will turn and lead you inside. You will then sit at their table for hours as they talk and talk and talk about everything except the death of their first grandchild.

Well, what else should they do? Petra was right on the phone: life goes on. It goes on and on and on. What is there, really, that anyone can say? It happened, that's all. It happened, and that's the most that any of you will ever understand about it.

It's dark by the time Ivan pulls onto the freeway. It's a stunning spring night, cool and warm all at once. The world feels electric until—*bang*—the freeway flashes white (a moment of daylight) and you are driving into icy walls of rain. In that second of brightness, you see something in the emergency lane: an animal, trotting against the traffic, towards the city. It's only a moment, but long enough for you to recognise his small determined face, his big pricked ears, his sleek body and the distinctive brush of his tail—held long and low and steady—steering him like a rudder through the squalling night. Dark again. Another lightening *bang*. The fox is gone, and the rain starts drumming harder.

You turn to Ivan—to tell him what you saw—but something in the hunch of him stops you. He has slowed right down. He is crouched over the steering wheel, his face close to the fogging windscreen as he tries to make out the white lines on the swishing, sparkling road. He refuses to return your gaze.

You look back out of your window. You rest your forehead against the cool glass and watch the huge soundproofing-walls of the freeway come and go with the pitch and flash of the storm.

Perhaps, you think, we are all born sleeping. Perhaps these things that happen to us—and to the people closest to us—are the only things that can ever, truly, wake us up.

Acknowledgements

This book was developed during the very confronting and disruptive time of the COVID-19 pandemic: thank you, Miami University Press, for publishing this book despite these troubles, and for continuing to value and support the Arts in a world that needs them more than ever.

Thanks, also, for recognising the elegant and powerful form of the novella with your annual competition and the beautifully-made books that result from it.

Thank you, Joe Squance, for choosing *Born Sleeping* to be published. Thanks Joe, Madysen George and Keith Tuma, for your insightful editing of the manuscript. Thanks, Brian Roley, for your advice during this process. Thank you, Amy Toland, for the huge amount of work you have put in to organising both the competition and the publication of this book. Thanks, also, to Jeff Clark, for designing this book and its cover.

Finally, I'd like to thank Eleanor and Paul Gildfind, Grace Yee, Kristen Robbins, and—of course—Igor. Thanks for being my first readers, and for your ongoing encouragement.

About the Author

H. C. Gildfind is an Australian writer who has published fiction, articles, and book reviews in Australia and overseas. She won an Australia Council Grant to complete a collection of short stories, *The Worry Front*, which was published in 2018 by Margaret River Press. Gildfind received an Australian postgraduate award to complete a PhD at the University of Melbourne, which enacted a creative reading of the relationship between Australian literature and history.